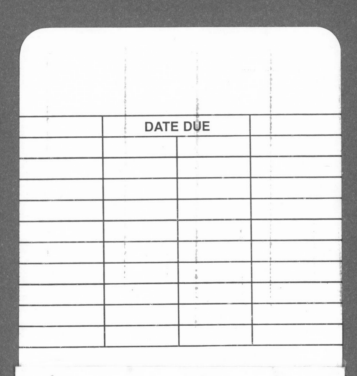

FLY, EAGLE, FLY!
AN AFRICAN TALE

Foreword by Archbishop Desmond Tutu

Fly, Eagle, Fly! is a charming and innovative adaptation of an African
tale attributed to a Ghanaian, James Kwegyir Aggrey—also known as
Aggrey of Africa. How frequently we have thought that we were chickens
destined to spend our lives limited to an earthly existence with limited
horizons, whereas we are made for something far more noble. We are
made for the sublime, the transcendent. We are not bound to this earth
and a humdrum existence but are made for something truly glorious: We
are not mere chickens but eagles destined to soar to sublime heights; we
are made for freedom and laughter and goodness and love and eternity,
despite all appearances to the contrary. We should be straining to
become what we have it in us to become; to gaze at the rising sun and
lift off and soar.

*Christopher Gregorowski is a wonderfully creative and gifted person,
and how deeply moving and poignant it is to think of what gave rise to
Fly, Eagle, Fly!—it was written for his dying child.*

Thank God for Christopher's giftedness—he has enriched us all.

To Josiah William and Gregory Colin
—C.G.

To the children of South Africa
—N.D.

Margaret K. McElderry Books
An imprint of Simon & Schuster
Children's Publishing Division
1230 Avenue of the Americas
New York, New York 10020

Book design by Niki Daly and Nina Barnett
The text of this book is set in Journal Text.
The illustrations were rendered in watercolors.

Printed in Hong Kong
By arrangement with The Inkman, Cape Town, South Africa.
Hand lettering by Andrew van der Merwe

10 9 8 7 6 5

Library of Congress Cataloging-in-Publication Data
Gregorowski, Christopher.
Fly, eagle, fly! : an African tale / retold by Christopher
Gregorowski; pictures by Niki Daly.—1st ed.   p.   cm.
Summary: A farmer finds an eagle and raises it to behave like a
chicken, until a friend helps the eagle learn to find its rightful
place in the sky.
ISBN: 0-689-82398-3
[1. Folklore—Africa.] I. Daly, Niki, ill. II. Title.
PZ8.1.G8645Fl   2000   398.2'096'04528942—dc21   98-45302

FLY, EAGLE, FLY!
AN AFRICAN TALE

retold by Christopher Gregorowski

pictures by Niki Daly

Margaret K. McElderry Books

A farmer went out one day to search for a lost calf.
The little herd boys had come back without it the evening
before. And that night there had been a terrible storm.

He went to the valley and searched. He searched by the riverbed. He searched among the reeds, behind the rocks, and in the rushing water.

He wandered over the hillside and through the dark and tangled forests where everything began, then out again along the muddy cattle tracks.

He searched in the long thatch grass, taller than his own head. He climbed the slopes of the high mountain with its rocky cliffs rising to the sky. He called out all the time, hoping that the calf might hear, but also because he felt so alone. His shouts echoed off the cliffs. The river roared in the valley below.

He climbed up a gully in case the calf had huddled there to escape the storm. And that was where he stopped. For there, on a ledge of rock, close enough to touch, he saw the most unusual sight—an eagle chick, very young, hatched from its egg a day or two before and then blown from its nest by the terrible storm.

He reached out and cradled it in both hands. He
would take it home and care for it. And home he went,
still calling, calling in case the calf might hear.

He was almost home when the children ran out to meet him. "The calf came back by itself!" they shouted. He was very pleased. He showed the eagle chick to his wife and children, then placed it carefully in the warm kitchen among the hens and chicks and under the watchful eye of the roosters.

"The eagle is the king of the birds," he said, "but we shall train it to be a chicken."

So the eagle lived among the chickens, learning their ways. His children called their friends to see the strange bird. For as it grew, living on the bits and pieces put out for the chickens, it began to look quite different from any chicken they had ever seen.

One day a friend dropped in for a visit. He and the farmer sat at the door of the kitchen hut, smoking their pipes. The friend saw the bird among the chickens. "Hey! That's not a chicken. It's an eagle!"

The farmer smiled at him and said, "Of course it's a chicken. Look—it walks like a chicken, it talks like a chicken, it eats like a chicken. It *thinks* like a chicken. Of course it's a chicken."

But the friend was not convinced. "I will show you that it is an eagle," he said.

"Go ahead," said the farmer.

The farmer's children helped his friend catch the bird. It was fairly heavy but he lifted it above his head and said: "You are not a chicken but an eagle. You belong not to the earth but to the sky. Fly, Eagle, fly!"

The bird stretched out its wings as the farmer and his family had seen it do before. But it looked about, saw the chickens feeding, and jumped down to scratch with them for food.

"I told you it was a chicken," the farmer said, and roared with laughter.

Next day the friend was back. "Farmer," he said, "I will prove to you that this is no chicken but an eagle. Bring me a ladder." With the large bird under one arm, he struggled up the slippery thatch of the tallest hut.

The farmer doubled over with laughter. "It eats chicken food. It thinks like a chicken. It *is* a chicken."

The friend, swaying on top of the hut, took the eagle's head, pointed it to the sky, and said: "You are not a chicken but an eagle. You belong not to the earth but to the sky. Fly, Eagle, fly!"

Again the great bird stretched out its wings. It trembled and the claws that clasped his hand opened. "Fly, Eagle, fly!" the man cried.

But the bird scrambled out of his hands, slid down the thatch, and sailed in among the chickens.

There was much laughter.

Very early next morning, on the third day, the farmer's dogs began to bark. A voice was calling outside in the darkness. The farmer ran to the door. It was his friend again. "Give me one more chance with the bird," he begged.

"Do you know the time? It's long before dawn. Are you crazy?"

"Come with me. Fetch the bird."

Reluctantly the farmer went into the kitchen, stepping over his sleeping children, and picked up the bird, which was fast asleep among the chickens. The two men set off, disappearing into the darkness.

"Where are we going?" asked the farmer sleepily.
"To the mountains where you found the bird."
"And why at this ridiculous time of the night?"
"So that our eagle may see the sun rise over the
mountain and follow it into the sky where it belongs."

They went into the valley and crossed the river, the friend leading the way. The bird was very heavy and too large to carry comfortably, but the friend insisted on taking it himself.

"Hurry," he said, "or the dawn will arrive before we do!"

The first light crept into the sky as they began to climb the mountain. Below them they could see the river snaking like a long, thin ribbon through the golden grasslands, the forest, and the veld, stretching down toward the sea. The wispy clouds in the sky were pink at first and then began to shimmer with a golden brilliance.

Sometimes their path was dangerous as it clung to the side of the mountain, crossing narrow shelves of rock and taking them into dark crevices and out again. They were both panting, especially the friend who was carrying the bird.

At last he said, "This will do." He looked down the cliff and saw the ground thousands of feet below. They were very near the top.

Carefully the friend carried the bird onto a ledge of rock. He set it down so that it looked toward the east, and began talking to it.

The farmer chuckled. "It talks only chickens' talk."

But the friend talked on, telling the bird about the sun, how it gives life to the world, how it reigns in the heavens, giving light to each new day.

"Look at the sun, Eagle. And when it rises, rise with it. You belong to the sky, not to the earth."

At that moment the sun's first rays shot out over the mountain, and suddenly the world was ablaze with light.

The golden sun rose majestically, dazzling them. The great bird stretched out its wings to greet the sun and feel the life-giving warmth on its feathers. The farmer was quiet. The friend said, "You belong not to the earth, but to the sky. Fly, Eagle, fly!"

He clambered back to the farmer.

All was silent. Nothing moved. The eagle's head stretched up; its wings stretched outwards; its legs leaned forward as its claws clutched the rock.

And then, without really moving, feeling the updraft of a wind more powerful than any man or bird, the great eagle leaned forward and was swept upward, higher and higher, lost to sight in the brightness of the rising sun, never again to live among the chickens.

A note from the author

I discovered this powerful parable in the biography of Aggrey of Africa, who visited West and South Africa in the 1920s from his teaching post in the USA. When Aggrey told this story, he closed by saying, "My people of Africa, we were created in the image of God, but men have made us think we are chickens, and we still think we are; but we are eagles. Don't be content with the food of chickens! Stretch forth your wings and fly!" At this, children would run excitedly around their playgrounds with arms outstretched like the wings of eagles. In 1981, when our seven-year-old daughter, Rosalind, was terminally ill, I wanted her to understand that we are all born to be eagles who are lifted up with the might of the Spirit—like the wind-borne flight of an eagle. So I wrote this story and dedicated it to her, setting it in the Transkei, where I worked among the Xhosa-speaking people as an Anglican priest. Now her two elder sisters have given us our first grandchildren, and I have dedicated this book to them: Josiah William and Gregory Colin.

A note from the illustrator

In 1982, when I first illustrated *Fly, Eagle, Fly!*, full-color illustrations were a luxury seldom seen in South African children's books. The first edition was published in South Africa as a two-color picture book. A few years later *Fly, Eagle, Fly!* went out of print, but it was not forgotten by the readers it had inspired. Now, as our new and precious democracy gives us wings to fly, a new edition with full-color pictures celebrates the flight of our many eagles—the children of South Africa, to whom I dedicate this book.